CHANGING TIMES

TREASURED HORSES COLLECTION™

titles in Large-Print Editions:

Changing Times

Colorado Summer

Kate's Secret Plan

Pride of the Green Mountains

Ride of Courage

Riding School Rivals

Spirit of the West

The Stallion of Box Canyon

CHANGING TIMES

The story of a Tennessee Walking Horse and the girl who proves that grown-ups don't always know best

Written by **Deborah Felder**
Illustrated by **Sandy Rabinowitz**
Cover Illustration by **Christa Keiffer**
Developed by Nancy Hall, Inc.

Gareth Stevens Publishing
MILWAUKEE

For a free color catalog describing Gareth Stevens' list of high-quality books and multimedia programs, call 1-800-542-2595 (USA) or 1-800-461-9120 (Canada). Gareth Stevens Publishing's Fax: (414) 225-0377.

Library of Congress Cataloging-in-Publication Data

Felder, Deborah G.
Changing times / written by Deborah Felder; illustrated by Sandy Rabinowitz; cover illustration by Christa Keiffer.
p. cm.
Originally published: Dyersville, Iowa: Ertl Co., 1996.
(Treasured horses collection)
Summary: In 1912, ten-year-old Lucy Gordon, living with her family in the foothills of Tennessee's Great Smoky Mountains, determines to prove that their Tennessee Walking Horse, Clipper, is worth far more than her father's new Model-T automobile.
ISBN 0-8368-2276-5 (lib. bdg.)
[1. Fathers and daughters—Fiction. 2. Tennessee walking horse—Fiction. 3. Horses—Fiction. 4. Automobiles—Fiction. 5. Tennessee—Fiction.] I. Rabinowitz, Sandy, ill. II. Title. III. Series: Treasured horses collection.
PZ7.F3356Ch 1999
[Fic]—dc21 98-44735

This edition first published in 1999 by
Gareth Stevens Publishing
1555 North RiverCenter Drive, Suite 201
Milwaukee, Wisconsin 53212 USA

© 1996 by Nancy Hall, Inc. First published by Scholastic Inc., New York, New York, by arrangement with Nancy Hall, Inc. and The ERTL Company.

Printed in the United States of America

1 2 3 4 5 6 7 8 9 03 02 01 00 99

CONTENTS

A Parade in Pine Bluff

T en-year-old Lucy Gordon carefully placed a crown made of flowers and pine cones on the head of Clipper, her Tennessee Walking Horse. "There," she said. "Now Clipper looks perfect!"

It was the first day of October in 1912, and it was Founder's Day in Pine Bluff, Tennessee. Founder's Day honored the founding of Pine Bluff in the 1800s by a pioneer named Joshua Sloan. The town, nestled in the foothills of the Great Smoky mountains, celebrated Founder's Day every year with a parade down Main Street.

Lucy had watched many Founder's Day parades, but this year's parade was extra special. For the first

time, Lucy's father, Dr. Phillip Gordon, was allowing her to march in the parade with Clipper. Lucy had hitched Clipper up to the Gordons' buggy. Then she and her best friend, Sarah Wilkes, had decorated the reins and the buggy with flowers and little bells.

Lucy stepped back and stood next to Sarah. She smiled with pleasure at Clipper. The dark coat of the handsome black gelding shone like satin in the bright sunshine, and the white stripe on his forehead peeked out under the crown of flowers and pine cones.

"Clipper really looks beautiful," Sarah said with a sigh. "I wish my folks would let me have my own horse. I'd have a Walker, too. One just as handsome and good-natured as Clipper."

"Clipper isn't just my horse," Lucy reminded Sarah as she stroked the Walker's velvety muzzle. "When Papa's not at the hospital, he uses Clipper almost every day to visit his patients, especially the ones who live in the hills. Papa's patients all say they start to feel better as soon as they hear Clipper clippity-clopping up to their cabins."

Lucy put her arms around Clipper's neck and gave him a hug. The Walker nickered softly and gently nuzzled Lucy's shoulder.

Ever since Lucy could remember, her father had made his rounds in the buggy. But Clipper was more than just a working horse. Lucy and Clipper had grown up together. She had learned to ride and drive him, and it had become her job to take care of him. Clipper was part of the family, and Lucy loved him very much.

"Hadn't you girls better be on your way?" a brisk voice suddenly asked from the porch steps. "The parade begins at ten o'clock sharp."

Lucy and Sarah turned to see Lucy's grandmother, Mary Gordon, coming down the steps of the big white farmhouse toward them.

Lucy's grandmother had grown up in Pine Bluff and had moved into the house as a young bride. Lucy's father had been born and raised there. When Lucy's mother died eight years ago, Lucy and her father had moved to Pine Bluff from Knoxville to live with Grandma Gordon.

Grandma Gordon was a tall, wiry woman, who seemed even taller to Lucy than she was because she always stood up so straight. She was always telling Lucy to stand up straight, too. Lucy was small and slender, like her mother.

"We're just going, Grandma," Lucy said. "But I wanted to talk to Papa first."

"Are you going to the parade this year, ma'am?" Sarah asked Grandma Gordon.

"Indeed I am not," Lucy's grandmother replied tartly. "I have been to more Founder's Day parades than I care to remember. And I have watched Amelia Sloan win the prize for the best float more years than I care to remember, too!"

Lucy and Sarah smiled at each other. What Grandma Gordon had said about Amelia Sloan was true. Every year, Mrs. Sloan, the wife of Joshua Sloan's great-grandson, drove a buckboard wagon in the parade. In the back of the wagon was a little log cabin and a sign advertising "Sloan and Sons Logging Company."

"Besides," Lucy's grandmother continued, "there's a great deal to do in the house today. I came outside because I wanted to be sure you girls were dressed up nicely and neatly. Now, stand up straight, don't fidget, and let me have a look at you."

Lucy and Sarah waited impatiently while Grandma Gordon looked them over with a critical eye. Both girls were wearing their second-best dresses, brown cotton stockings, and brown ankle boots made of soft leather. Lucy's blond curls and Sarah's long black braids were pulled back and kept in place by big bows. Lucy's bow was blue to match her eyes and her dress.

"Well, you both look very nice," Grandma Gordon finally said with a smile and an approving nod. "And

I'm glad to see that you remembered to bring a clean handkerchief. You, too, Sarah Wilkes."

Lucy breathed a sigh of relief. She knew how strict her grandmother could be about neatness. And manners, too.

"May I go to see Papa now, please, Grandma?" Lucy asked.

"Yes, of course you may, but be quick, child," Grandma Gordon replied. "He's in his office. Be sure to knock on the door before you go in."

Lucy nodded and ran up the porch steps into the house. The house was quiet except for the ticking of the big grandfather clock in the hallway. Lucy walked through the parlor to her father's office and knocked on the door. A cheerful voice called out, "Come in!"

Lucy stepped into the office and saw her father sitting behind his big oak desk. Beyond the desk was the door that led to his examining room.

Lucy's father was hunched over the desk studying a medical journal and writing notes on a pad of yellow paper. He ran his hand through his thick brown hair, making it stand up on end, and wrote down another word. Then he looked up at Lucy and smiled.

"I've been reading about vitamins, my dear, vitamins!" he said, pointing at the journal with the tip of his fountain pen. His brown eyes beneath his steel-rimmed glasses shone with excitement. "It's the very latest discovery in medicine. Think of all the children who can be made strong and healthy now because of vitamins! I just hope I can convince Dr. Beasley and Dr. Graham how important vitamins are. Those two are so old-fashioned."

He put down his pen and folded his hands. "But I know you didn't come in here to listen to a lecture on vitamins," he said kindly. His eyes twinkled. "You haven't come to ask me about the surprise, have you?"

"The surprise?" Lucy said in a puzzled tone. Then she remembered. Last night at dinner Papa had told her and Grandma Gordon that a "surprise" was arriving at the house the next day. But Lucy had forgotten about it. Driving Clipper in the parade was all she cared about right now.

"I know you and your grandmother can't wait to find out what it is," Papa said. "But if I told you, it wouldn't be a surprise, would it? All I'll say," he added in a mysterious tone, "is that it's a modern machine that will help me in my work. But you and your grandmother will love it, too."

"Papa, I just wanted to ask . . ." Lucy began.

"Now, don't be impatient, Lucy," Papa broke in with a smile. "The surprise will be here waiting for you when you get home from the parade."

"Um, that's wonderful, Papa," Lucy said. "But I wanted to ask you if you're coming to watch Clipper and me in the parade. Clipper will look so beautiful. I know you'll be proud of him."

"I'm afraid I can't come to the parade this year, my dear," Papa said in a regretful tone as he picked up his pen. "But I need to finish these notes before our surprise arrives. You and Clipper have a good time at the parade." He dipped his pen in the inkwell and began writing on the pad of paper again.

"We will," Lucy said with a sigh. "Good-bye, then, Papa."

Without looking up from the pad of paper, Dr. Gordon waved good-bye to his daughter.

Lucy turned and left the office, gently closing the door behind her. She felt very disappointed. She didn't mind so much that Grandma wasn't going to the parade. Grandma Gordon never went. But Lucy and her father had gone to the parade together every year since Lucy was a little girl. Why does this dumb surprise have to come today? Lucy thought as she walked back through the parlor. The surprise seemed to be all her father cared about. That and vitamins, whatever *they* were.

When Lucy got outside, she saw that Sarah was fixing a banner to the back of the buggy. The girls had made the banner the day before. In big red letters it read, "We love Pine Bluff, U.S.A."

"We need to get going," Sarah said. "It's a quarter to ten. If we don't leave now, we might end up last in line with the street sweeper!"

Clipper was busy munching tufts of grass. Lucy patted him on the neck. "No more nibbling now, Clipper," she said. "It's time to go."

Lucy stepped into the buggy and unhooked the reins from the hook on the buggy top. She sat on the black seat and gripped the reins in her small hands. When Sarah had settled herself on the seat beside her, Lucy lightly slapped the reins across Clipper's back, making the little bells ring. Then she said in a gentle but firm voice, "Walk on, Clip."

Clipper picked up his ears and immediately moved forward. Lucy guided him out of the front yard, then turned him onto the broad gravel road that led into town. Clipper broke into the graceful, gliding, running walk his breed is famous for. His head nodded in time with the movement of his pace. Clipper's walk made the bells on his reins jingle cheerfully, and soon Lucy began to feel more cheerful, too.

The morning mountain mist had began to lift, and soon Lucy could see the spire of the church in the center of town. After they had passed the

schoolhouse, they reached the crowd. Most were
dressed up like pioneers from the 1800s, in calico
dresses and sunbonnets or buckskin shirts and pants.
They were on horseback or driving buckboard wagons
or buggies. Many of the wagons had been decorated
to advertise different businesses in Pine Bluff.

Lucy spotted a place in line between the Pine Bluff
Boy Scout troop and Lavinia Atkins, the mayor's wife.
She pulled up on the reins to slow Clipper and wedged
him and the buggy in behind Mrs. Atkins.

"Move back, boys," Lucy heard Mr. Simpson, the
scoutmaster, say. "We need to make room for the girls
and their fine-looking horse and buggy."

Mrs. Atkins turned her head to see who was
behind her. She was a heavyset, red-faced woman
wearing a long pink gingham dress and a pink
sunbonnet. She was mounted sidesaddle on her
chestnut mare, Misty. She did not look pleased to see
Lucy, Sarah, and especially Clipper.

"The idea!" she said in a huffy tone. "Placing a
horse and buggy behind Misty and me! It's simply not
dignified. As the first lady of Pine Bluff, I *always* march
between our scouts and the drum and bugle corps!"

"We're sorry, ma'am," Lucy said in a small voice.
"But this was the only place we could find."

"The idea," Mrs. Atkins repeated, turning away.

"Don't mind her," Sarah whispered to Lucy. "I bet she's just jealous because Clipper and the buggy look so beautiful. Now everyone will be watching us and not her!"

Just then, the Pine Bluff town band, which was standing at the front of the line, struck up a march.

"It's starting," Lucy said excitedly. She gripped Clipper's reins and waited for Mrs. Atkins and Misty to move forward.

When they finally did, Lucy urged Clipper into a walk, making sure that the reins were just taut enough so that the Walker kept a slow, steady pace.

Soon they began to pass the crowds of cheering, waving townspeople lined up along both sides of Main Street. Lucy and Sarah smiled and waved at the crowd. Most of them were people they knew, but others had come from neighboring towns to watch the parade.

"This is fun," Lucy said after they had waved to Sarah's parents and two older brothers, who were standing on the steps of the Wilkes's General Store. "I can't wait to tell Papa all about it!"

A moment later, they reached the judging stand, a platform where the mayor, a state senator, the senator's wife, and Marcus Sloan sat. Marcus Sloan was the great-grandson of the founder of Pine Bluff,

Joshua Sloan. The judges smiled, nodded to one another, and clapped as the girls and Clipper drove past.

"Did you see that?" Sarah said, her round face rosy with excitement. "They liked us! Maybe we'll win the blue ribbon for the best float this year."

"That would be wonderful," Lucy agreed. She imagined herself driving home with the blue ribbon around Clipper's neck. Wouldn't Papa and Grandma Gordon be proud then!

Lucy was about to follow Mrs. Atkins and Misty across Church Street, when she heard the sound of a car horn. She glanced to her left and was surprised to see a black Model-T car barreling down Church Street toward them.

"Who can that be?" Sarah asked. "The only car in Pine Bluff belongs to the Sloans, and they're all at the parade."

Lucy shrugged and said, "I don't know who it is." But as the car came closer, she and Sarah could see that a woman was driving it. The woman was wearing a long coat and a big hat that was kept in place by a gauzy scarf. Driving goggles covered her eyes.

The woman slowed the car down at the intersection and stopped. Then she began to back up. As she did, the car let out a loud backfire.

Startled by the noise, Clipper jumped forward and then broke into a fast running walk, heading straight for Mrs. Atkins and Misty!

Lucy Is Very Surprised

hoa, Clipper!" Lucy cried out desperately as the buggy sped forward. "Whoa, boy!" She pulled up on the reins with all her might. They were coming closer and closer to Mrs. Atkins and Misty.

"I can't look," Sarah said with a groan, covering her face with her hands.

Mrs. Atkins turned her head. Her eyes opened wide at the sight of Clipper bearing down on her, his head nodding up and down and the crown of flowers and pine cones hanging over one ear. She let out a loud scream.

At that moment, Lucy yanked hard on the left rein. Clipper jerked up his head and turned away from Mrs.

Atkins and Misty. But the buggy brushed close by them, startling Misty. The chestnut mare reared up, sending Mrs. Atkins tumbling to the ground. Misty cantered off toward the drum and bugle corps. The notes of the fanfare they were playing died away as they scattered in all directions. Out of the corner of her eye, Lucy could see Misty heading in the direction of the Atkins's home farther down Main Street.

By now, Clipper had slowed down. With another "Whoa, boy," Lucy brought him to a stop as she glanced over her shoulder and saw that the car was gone. She and Sarah jumped out of the buggy and rushed over to Mrs. Atkins to see if she was all right. They reached her at the same time as Mr. Atkins. With him was Dr. Beasley, a plump, older man with white hair and a white beard.

Mrs. Atkins was sitting on the ground. Her face and dress were covered with dust from the road, and her sunbonnet was hanging over one shoulder. Her elaborate hairdo had come loose, and hairpins were sticking out of the back of it.

"Are you injured, Lavinia?" Mr. Atkins asked anxiously. He was a short, thin man who always seemed afraid of his wife.

"Of course I'm injured!" Mrs. Atkins bellowed, looking up at him. "Didn't you see what happened to me? The disgrace!" She coughed and waved a small cloud of dust away from her face. "Well, just don't stand there, Henry," she snapped. "Help me up!"

Mr. Atkins helped his wife to her feet. She turned to face Lucy and Sarah, her dusty face even redder than usual.

"If you can't control that horse of yours, Lucy Gordon, you shouldn't have him in the parade," she said angrily. "That horse is a menace!"

"But it wasn't my fault, Mrs. Atkins. Or Clipper's fault, either," Lucy insisted. "It was the car. Clipper got scared when it made that loud noise."

Mrs. Atkins looked down at her. "Don't you dare sass me, young lady. Car or no car, I intend to tell your father and your grandmother what you and your horse did to me!"

"Now, now, Lavinia," Mr. Atkins said, timidly patting his wife's hand. "Don't upset yourself so. Lucy didn't mean to be rude, I'm sure. And, after all, accidents do happen."

"They don't happen to *me*, Henry Atkins," Mrs. Atkins said sharply. She put her hand to her head. "I declare, I'm feeling faint, quite faint. Doctor! Doctor!"

"Yes, Mrs. Atkins, I'm here," Dr. Beasley said soothingly. "Now, why don't you let me take you home." He led the mayor's wife away.

Lucy thought that Mr. Atkins looked a little relieved to see them go.

"Well, girls, you'd better take your places again," Mr. Atkins said. "Then the parade can proceed once more." He scurried off.

"Do you think Mrs. Atkins is really hurt?" Lucy asked anxiously as she and Sarah hurried back to Clipper and the buggy.

"If you ask me, the only thing hurt was her pride," Sarah said. "She had no call to yell at you like that, Lucy. You did a fine job slowing Clipper down. It wasn't your fault he ran away like that. It was an accident, like Mr. Atkins said."

"I know," Lucy said, stepping up to Clipper. The Walker was nibbling at the flowers of his crown, which had fallen onto the ground.

Lucy stroked Clipper's neck comfortingly. "You couldn't help it if that car scared you, could you, Clip?" she whispered. "Cars are dumb. I'd much rather have you than a noisy, smelly, old car any day."

Just then, she heard the drum and bugle corps begin to play again. Clipper raised his head and pricked up his ears. Lucy gave him a quick kiss, then picked up the crown. "There's no use putting this back on your head," she said with a sigh. "The flowers are all gone, and most of the pine cones."

But Clipper's crown wasn't the only decoration that had come undone during his run. The flowers on the reins and buggy had either fallen off or were drooping, and the banner that read "We Love Pine Bluff, U.S.A." was trailing on the ground, torn and dusty. Only the little bells had stayed put.

"Well, I guess we're not going to win any blue ribbons today," Sarah said, after she and Lucy had gotten back into the buggy.

Lucy nodded. She took hold of the reins and steered Clipper back into their place in the parade. Slowly and silently they marched the rest of the way down Main Street toward the village green, where the parade ended. This time, neither Lucy nor Sarah felt much like smiling and waving to the crowd.

Lucy was worried. What if Mrs. Atkins does tell Papa about Clipper and the buggy making her fall off Misty? she thought. Lucy had just barely been able to convince him that she was old enough to drive the buggy by herself. Now Papa might never let her drive Clipper again.

When they reached the village green, Lucy turned Clipper and the buggy around so that they were facing back the way they had come. A little while later, the Pine Bluff fire wagon arrived at the green. It was the last float of the parade. The marchers and parade watchers began to mill around the little park, greeting friends and relatives. Lucy and Sarah spotted Sarah's parents coming toward them. Mr. Wilkes was a tall, muscular man with a pleasant face and a ready smile. Sarah's mother was short and plump like her daughter, with the same black hair and sparkling black eyes.

"We saw Clipper take off after Mrs. Atkins," Mr. Wilkes told the girls. "We started to come after you, but by then Lucy had stopped Clipper, and we could see that you two were all right."

Lucy and Sarah got out of the buggy. Lucy stood by Clipper and held onto his bridle to keep him from eating the grass. In Pine Bluff it was against the law for animals to graze on the village green.

"That was a foolish thing to do, driving a car almost into the middle of a parade like that," Mrs. Wilkes declared. "Did you girls see who it was?"

"I doubt if Lucy and Sarah had much time to introduce themselves, Kate," Mr. Wilkes said with a laugh.

"It wasn't anyone we know," Sarah told her parents. "And it was a woman."

"A woman driving a car," Mrs. Wilkes said, shaking her head. "Well, well, what next, I'd like to know!"

At that moment, Lucy saw Mr. Atkins and Marcus Sloan step up onto the bandstand. A hush fell over the crowd as the mayor thanked those who had marched in the parade and the spectators. Then he held up a blue ribbon with a medal at the end of it and cleared his throat.

"And now, without further ado, I would like to award the medal for the best float in the parade," Lucy heard him say. "It goes to Pine Bluff's own Amelia Sloan!"

There was cheering and applause as Marcus Sloan's wife, Amelia, made her way, blushing and smiling, up the steps of the bandstand.

"Big surprise," Sarah said, rolling her eyes.

Lucy stroked Clipper's muzzle. "Never mind, Clip," she said to him in a soothing tone. "You were still the handsomest horse in the whole parade."

Mrs. Wilkes put her arm around Lucy. "I know you're feeling disappointed, honey," she said gently. "We could see that you and Sarah worked very hard to make Clipper and the buggy into a special float."

"Why don't you come over and have lunch with us?" Sarah suggested. "Can she, Mama?"

"Of course," Sarah's mother replied with a smile.

"Thank you," Lucy said, smiling back at Sarah and her parents. "But Papa and Grandma are expecting me at home."

She got back into the buggy and took hold of the

reins. "See you in school on Monday," she said to
Sarah as she lightly slapped the reins across Clipper's
back. Sarah nodded and waved.

Lucy drove out of the crowd and headed back
down Main Street. When she had left the crowd of
people behind, she urged Clipper into a faster gait, the
running walk. Clipper was happy to obey. He moved
quickly, with a smooth, flowing pace. As always, his
head nodded up and down, and his ears swung back
and forth in rhythm with his head. It was the same
gait he had moved into when he had almost run into
Mrs. Atkins earlier. But there was no danger of Clipper
crashing into anyone on the deserted road.

They were about a quarter of a mile from home
when Lucy suddenly spotted someone walking down
the road toward them. As Lucy came closer, she could
see that it was a short, pretty woman with shining red
hair. The woman was carrying a coat over her right
arm and swinging a big hat in her left hand. A gauzy
scarf was draped around her neck. As Lucy and
Clipper passed by, the woman glanced over at them
and smiled.

"Where have I seen her before?" Lucy murmured.
"I know! She was the woman who was driving that
car. I wonder who she is."

They were quickly approaching the house. Lucy

saw her father and Grandma Gordon coming down the porch steps. And she was surprised to see something else. Sitting in front of the house was a black Model-T car, just like the car the red-haired woman had been driving earlier.

Lucy slowed Clipper down and turned him onto the path that led to the barn. Then she brought him to a stop. She got out of the buggy and walked over to her father and grandmother.

"Well, Lucy, how do you like your surprise?" Lucy's father asked as he gazed at the car, his thumbs in his vest pockets.

Lucy's eyes widened. "Papa, do you mean . . . " She was too astonished to finish her sentence.

"That's right," her father said with a broad grin. "We are now the proud owners of a Model-T Ford!"

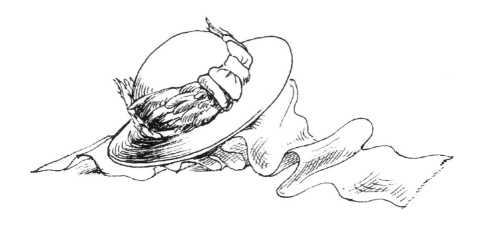

The New Car

Lucy stared at the Model T parked in front of the house. She couldn't believe that it really belonged to them.

"It's a beauty, isn't it?" Lucy's father said proudly, as he stepped up to the car and ran his hand along the Model T's shining metal sides. "I saw an ad in the Pine Bluff *Gazette* for the car. I wrote to the box number and received a reply from the car's owner, Miss Maggie Sullivan. She was moving to Pine Bluff and wanted to sell the car." He turned to Lucy. "You probably passed Miss Sullivan on the road while you were driving home from the parade. She's a pretty woman with red hair."

Lucy nodded. "Yes, I saw her," she said. "But I don't understand something, Papa. Why do we need a car? We always use Clipper and the buggy."

"I've been thinking about buying a car for a long time," her father explained. "A car will get me to my patients more quickly and efficiently. Especially now that there are so many new logging roads in the hills around town."

"That's all well and good, Phillip," Grandma Gordon said. "But do you know how to drive this contraption?"

"No," Lucy's father admitted. "But Miss Sullivan has promised to teach me. It won't take me long to learn, I'm sure. Then I can teach you, Mother."

Grandma Gordon shook her head. "No thank you, Phillip," she said firmly. "I do not intend to either drive or ride in that tin lizzie or any other. A horse and buggy is good enough for me!"

Lucy remembered hearing the boys at school call Model T's "tin lizzies." She knew it was a nickname for a car, but she didn't know why.

Before she could ask Papa and Grandma Gordon, her father said, "Now, Mother, you mustn't be so old-fashioned. Cars are the way of the future, as Mr. Henry Ford, the designer and builder of the Model T, has often said. Soon everyone in America will own a car."

"Well, begging Mr. Henry Ford's pardon, the only future event I care to think about right now is getting lunch on the table," Grandma Gordon said crisply. "Lucy, you'd better see to Clipper."

She looked over at Clipper and the buggy, and a surprised expression crossed her face. "Good gracious child," she exclaimed. "How did that buggy and those reins become so bedraggled?"

"Something scared Clipper at the parade, and he broke into a run," Lucy told her. "But I was able to slow him down." It wasn't the whole truth, but it wasn't really a lie either, Lucy decided. She looked over at her father to see if he had heard what she had said. He was busy cleaning off a spot on the car with his handkerchief.

Grandma Gordon seemed to be satisfied with Lucy's explanation. She nodded and went back into the house. Lucy felt relieved. Now if only Mrs. Atkins forgets to tell Papa what happened to her, she thought, as she took hold of Clipper's bridle.

She led Clipper down the path into the red barn at the back of the house. The barn was used as a garage for the buggy and as a stable and tack room for Clipper. Lucy wondered if they would park the car in the barn, too.

After Lucy unhitched Clipper from the buggy, she

unbuckled the reins from his bridle. She gently removed Clipper's bridle and harness and brushed him down well to remove the sweat and dust from his coat. She slipped his halter over his head and attached the lead line. Then she led Clipper outside to the water trough under the cottonwood tree. Next to the trough was a pump that attached to a well deep in the ground. Lucy pushed the pump handle up and down until the water began to gush into the trough.

When Clipper had finished his drink of water, Lucy turned him out in the paddock, a fenced-in area of a meadow next to the barn. Rising up behind the barn and the paddock was a big hill forested with pine trees.

Lucy leaned against the gate and watched Clipper graze, his high-set silken tail twitching gently as he nibbled contentedly at the grass. As Lucy looked at him, she suddenly thought of something, and her eyes lit up.

"Now that Papa has the car, he won't need to use Clipper," she said to herself. "That means that I'll be able to spend more time riding him after school and on weekends." But at the same time, Lucy felt a little sad that soon she wouldn't be riding in the buggy with her father when he visited his patients. Those buggy rides had always been special times for both of them. Lucy tried to imagine what it would be like to ride in the car with her father while he made his rounds. She shook her head and sighed. She just knew it wouldn't be the same.

Suddenly Lucy heard a screen door slam and Grandma Gordon call out "Lucy!" She turned and ran past the barn to the house. Her grandmother was standing outside the kitchen door, wiping her hands on her apron.

"I'm sorry I was so long, Grandma," Lucy said breathlessly as she followed her grandmother into the kitchen. "Do you need any help?"

"You can take the milk out to the table," Grandma Gordon replied, nodding at a glass pitcher sitting on the counter. She untied her apron, draped it over the back of the rocking chair, and picked up a platter of chicken sandwiches.

Lucy eyed the sandwiches hungrily. They had been made with Grandma Gordon's home-baked bread, and Lucy knew they would taste delicious.

When they entered the dining room, Lucy saw that her father was already sitting in his place at the head of the table. He was glancing at the Pine Bluff *Gazette*. Lucy carefully put the pitcher down on the table and sat in the chair to the right of her father. Grandma Gordon sat in the chair opposite Lucy.

"I see here that a fellow named Clarence Birdseye is working on a way to freeze food so that it will last longer," Lucy's father said. He grinned over the top of the page at Lucy and her grandmother. "Frozen food. What a wonderful idea!"

"Put the paper away, Phillip," Grandma Gordon said sharply. "How many times do I have to remind you that there's no reading at the table."

Lucy bit her lip to keep from laughing. She always thought it was funny when Grandma Gordon scolded her grown-up son as if he were the same age as Lucy.

"Sorry, Mother," Lucy's father said. He promptly folded up the paper and placed it on the floor next to his chair. "Lucy, would you pass the potato salad, please?"

As Lucy picked up the bowl and handed it to her father, she asked, "Papa, why do some people call Model T's 'tin lizzies?'"

"Well, people used to believe that Model T's were made of tin," Lucy's father explained. "But they're really made of a different metal. The name 'lizzie' is an all-around nickname for a family's maid. Some families have a maid who does all kinds of household chores. Instead of someone saying that they have a maid, they might say they have a 'lizzie.' A Model T does many different kinds of work, too. Why, I've heard that some folks even use it to plow fields and haul in the hay."

Lucy reached for another chicken sandwich. "I didn't know that farmers used Model T's," she said. "I thought you had to be rich to own a car, like the Sloans."

"Model T's do cost a lot of money," her father agreed. "Miss Sullivan told me hers was a gift from her father, Senator Sullivan, and she still finds it expensive to maintain. That's why she's selling."

"Then how can we afford it?" Lucy asked.

"I made a very good deal with Miss Sullivan. I was able to pay her a discounted price for the car by agreeing to give her Clipper and the buggy. She'll be taking them in two weeks."

Lucy stared at her father in stunned silence. All of a sudden, the delicious chicken sandwich tasted like sawdust in her mouth. She swallowed hard. "But Papa," she said, her voice trembling, "you can't give Clipper away. You know how much I love him. Please don't do it, Papa!"

"We must keep up with the times, Lucy," her father insisted. "New inventions and discoveries are changing our lives in wonderful ways. The automobile is a perfect example. Believe me, once you've taken a few spins in our car, you'll feel just as I do—that the days of horses and buggies are gone for good."

"No, Papa, I could never feel that way about Clipper," Lucy whispered miserably, looking down at her plate. She pushed the sandwich aside.

Dr. Gordon reached over and patted his daughter's hand. "Trust me, my dear," he said. "In time you'll see the wisdom of my decision." He went back to eating his lunch.

Lucy knew that as far as her father was concerned, the subject was closed. He had made up his mind, and there was nothing she could do about it.

She raised her head and looked at her grandmother. Grandma Gordon gave her a tender look of pity, as if she understood exactly how Lucy was feeling. It made Lucy want to burst into tears.

"May I be excused, Grandma?" Lucy asked in a small voice. "I'm not very hungry."

"Yes, dear, you may," Grandma Gordon said quietly.

Lucy managed to hold back her tears until she had left the house and run over to the paddock. When Clipper saw her coming, he softly whinnied a welcome and rushed over to her. Lucy climbed up onto the second rung of the fence and threw her arms around his neck. Then she began to cry.

"It's all *her* fault," Lucy sobbed into Clipper's mane. "She's the one who brought that dumb car here. And now she's going to take you away from me. I hope I never, *ever* have to see that awful Maggie Sullivan again!"

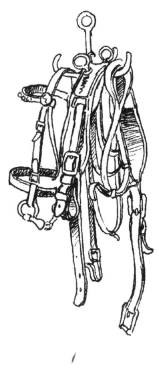

CHAPTER FOUR

Miss Maggie Sullivan

The next time Lucy brought up the subject of Clipper was on Monday morning. She had been quiet about Clipper all day on Sunday in the hope that her father would change his mind about trading him away to Miss Sullivan.

But he hadn't.

"I'm sorry, Lucy," he said firmly, as they sat around the table at breakfast. "My mind is made up. We need the car, and we don't need Clipper. I'm afraid that's the end of the discussion."

There was an uncomfortable silence. Lucy's father took a last sip of his coffee, stood up, and buttoned up his suit jacket. "Well, I'd better be on my way," he said in a cheerful voice. "It's such a fine day, I think I'll walk to the hospital this morning." With that, he turned and left the dining room.

"Grandma, isn't there anything we can do to change Papa's mind?" Lucy pleaded.

Grandma Gordon put down her coffee cup with a sigh. "Your father is the most stubborn man in creation," she said, shaking her head. "He always was, even as a boy. He'll stick to his decision, and neither you nor I will be able to talk him out of it."

"But don't you want to keep Clipper and the buggy, too?" Lucy asked.

"Yes I do, Lucy," Grandma Gordon replied quietly. "But your father is the head of this household, and we must go by his wishes. Now it's time you were off to school."

It's not fair, Lucy thought, as she left the room and trudged into the front hall. Nobody cares how I feel about Clipper. Nobody at all. She picked up her books, slate, and lunch pail from the hall table and stepped out of the house.

But instead of turning onto the road toward the schoolhouse, Lucy headed down the path that led to the paddock. She wanted to spend as much time with Clipper as she could while he still belonged to her.

When Lucy reached the paddock, she saw that Clipper already had company. A big yellow dog was pawing the ground, then running back and forth outside the paddock, trying to tease Clipper into chasing him. The dog's name was Andy Jackson, and he belonged to Charlie Turner, a handyman who lived in a log cabin in the hills. Mr. Turner had named Andy Jackson after the seventh president of the United States, Andrew Jackson, who had lived in Tennessee.

Clipper looked calmly over the fence at Andy Jackson dodging and running. He whinnied softly and shook his head so that his mane fluttered. The dog sat on his haunches and cocked his head to one side. He looked as if he were puzzled by Clipper's behavior.

"What's the matter, Andy Jackson," Lucy said with a laugh. "Won't Clipper play with you?"

"Your Clipper has better things to do than to chase around after a dog," a voice said behind her. "Tennessee Walkers are too quiet and sensible to let a dog rile them up, even in fun. That's one of the things that makes them so special."

Lucy turned and saw Charlie Turner standing a few feet away. He was a big man with bushy blond hair and a thick beard streaked with white. No one knew his real age, but Grandma Gordon once guessed that he was about fifty-five. As usual, he was carrying a large bag of tools slung across his shoulder. Mr. Turner went from house to house in Pine Bluff mending fences, repairing doors, and fixing just about anything else that needed fixing. Everyone in Pine Bluff knew and liked Charlie Turner.

"Clipper *is* special," Lucy agreed. Then she added in a sad tone, "But he's not going to be my horse much longer, Mr. Turner. Papa traded him away for a Model-T car. In two weeks, he'll be gone."

"Well, now, that is a shame," Mr. Turner said, shaking his head. "You must be feeling real bad."

Lucy nodded. Then she suddenly thought of something. "Maybe Clipper and I could run away," she said, her eyes lighting up. "We could go into the hills where no one would ever find us."

"You could do that," Mr. Turner said slowly. "But it might be kind of hard on Clipper, not having a nice warm stable to sleep in and a good-tasting pail of oats and bran to eat."

"I guess you're right," Lucy said with a sigh. "It was a dumb idea."

"I wouldn't give up hope if I were you," Mr. Turner said kindly. "Two weeks is a long time. Anything can happen in two weeks." He shifted the bag of tools to his other shoulder, adding, "I'd better go see if your grandma wants that squeaky screen door repaired. And I reckon you'd better be on your way to school." He gave her an encouraging smile and headed off toward the house.

Lucy started up the path. Then she stopped and looked back at Clipper. As she did, she saw a sight that made her smile. Clipper was touching noses with Andy Jackson through the fence.

Lucy wanted to stay and watch Clipper and Andy Jackson a little longer, but she knew that if she did, she would be late for school. With a reluctant sigh, she turned and continued up the path to the road.

As she hurried down the road, she suddenly remembered that there was going to be a new teacher at school. The students' former teacher, Miss Bremer, had gone out West to be married. Lucy wondered what their new teacher would be like.

She was halfway to the schoolhouse when she heard the school bell begin to clang. The teacher rang it before school and after recess to alert the students to come into the schoolhouse and take their seats.

Lucy clutched her books and lunch pail tightly and began to run. She bounded up the schoolhouse steps into the building just as the bell stopped ringing. The big room was filled with the sounds of children talking and laughing. Lucy quickly made her way down the center aisle to the wooden double desk she shared with Sarah.

"I made it just in time!" she said to Sarah, as she plunked her books and slate down on the desk and shoved her lunch pail underneath her seat. "What is the new teacher like?"

Lucy looked up at the front of the room and gasped in surprise. There, writing the name "Margaret Sullivan" on the blackboard, was the short, pretty woman with shining red hair piled high on her head. At first, Lucy couldn't believe her eyes. "It can't be the same woman," she whispered. "It just can't be." But when the woman turned around and smiled, Lucy immediately recognized her.

"That's the woman who scared Clipper with her car at the parade," Lucy told Sarah in a low voice. "Remember?"

Sarah nodded. "I remember her now. I can't believe she's our new teacher!"

"But that's not all," Lucy went on. "Papa bought her car, and he traded away Clipper to her as part of the price."

Sarah stared at Lucy in horror. "Lucy!" she exclaimed. "That's terrible!"

"I know," Lucy said, choking back tears.

Just then, Miss Sullivan picked up a ruler and gently tapped it against her big desk. "All right, children," she called out in a pleasant voice. "Settle down now, please." She tapped the ruler again, and after a minute, the room was silent.

"My name is Miss Margaret Sullivan, and I'll be your teacher for the rest of the year," Miss Sullivan said, smiling warmly. "We'll begin our lessons in a little while. But first I'd like to start getting acquainted with you." She picked up a notebook and opened it. "When I call your name, please stand up and answer 'Here' or 'Present.'"

She began with the six-year-olds who were in the first class. They were the youngest children in the school and sat in the front of the room. Lucy couldn't help but notice how gentle and patient Miss Sullivan acted toward them, especially when it was shy little Betsy Baker's turn. But Lucy didn't want to think about how nice her new teacher was acting. She had vowed to dislike Miss Sullivan, and she didn't want anything to change her mind.

Finally, Miss Sullivan started to read the names of the sixth class. When she called out Lucy's name, she asked, "Are you Dr. Gordon's daughter?"

"Yes, ma'am," Lucy said, standing up. Then she added quickly, "Present, ma'am."

Miss Sullivan's blue eyes lit up. "I'm so happy to meet you, Lucy," she said enthusiastically. "And I'm looking forward to seeing you again at your house after school. I'm giving your father his first driving lesson today, you know."

Lucy's face turned red with embarrassment. "No, ma'am, I didn't know that," she muttered.

"He seems a very eager student. I hope you take after him, Lucy," Miss Sullivan said with a smile.

"Yes, ma'am," she replied, as she slowly sat down again. She felt as if everyone in the school was staring at her. Out of the corner of her eye, she saw Sarah give her a sympathetic look.

Why did she have to make such a big fuss over me like that? Lucy thought miserably. In front of the whole school, too! And does she really have to come over to my house?

The morning dragged on. At recess, Lucy and Sarah took their lunch pails over to their favorite spot by the brook. Even though it was October and the leaves were beginning to change, it was still warm enough for Lucy and her schoolmates to eat and play outside at recess.

Lucy and Sarah settled themselves on a big flat rock and opened their lunch pails. A moment later, they were joined by three of their classmates, Emily

Sloan, Faith Baker, and Carrie Deakins.

"Well, Lucy Gordon, how does it feel to be teacher's pet?" Emily asked sweetly, as she spread her sweater on another rock and daintily sat down. Emily was the daughter of Marcus and Amelia Sloan.

"I'm not teacher's pet," Lucy said hotly. "I don't even like Miss Sullivan. You girls were at the parade. You saw how her car scared Clipper and made him almost run into Mrs. Atkins. It was all Miss Sullivan's fault!"

Then she suddenly noticed that Miss Sullivan was standing near them. She looked at Lucy for a moment with a puzzled, hurt expression. Embarrassed, Lucy looked down at the uneaten sandwich in her lap. When she raised her eyes again a moment later, she saw Miss Sullivan walking back to the schoolhouse.

"Well, I like Miss Sullivan," Faith said, picking an apple out of her lunch pail. "I think she's much nicer and prettier than Miss Bremer."

"But you don't know what else she did," Lucy insisted. She told them about the trade of Clipper for the Model T.

"That's simply awful," Carrie said, when Lucy had finished. "I don't know what I'd do if my folks made me give up Lily." Lily was Carrie's dapple-gray mare.

"I think you're making a big fuss over nothing,"

Emily said with a sniff. "Cars are much better than horses. Who wants to drive a poky old horse around when you can ride in a big, shiny, fast car?" She brushed the crumbs from her skirt, then got up and stepped down to the brook to wash her hands.

"That's Emily Sloan," Sarah said, shaking her head. "Just because her folks are rich, she thinks she knows everything."

"Well, she doesn't know anything about Clipper, that's for sure," Lucy said. "If she did, I bet she'd definitely change her mind about cars!"

The girls continued eating and talking until the school bell rang for the end of recess. Lucy and her friends shut their lunch pails and hurried back into the schoolhouse.

Lucy and her classmates spent the afternoon solving math problems Miss Sullivan had written on the blackboard. Lucy liked math, and she worked out the problems quickly. Miss Sullivan came over to check the answers she had written with chalk on her slate.

"That's very good work, Lucy," the teacher said with a smile.

Lucy was surprised. She hadn't expected Miss Sullivan to be so nice after what she had overheard Lucy say down by the brook at recess.

When school was over, Miss Sullivan caught up to Lucy outside the schoolhouse door.

"I thought that since we were both going to your house, we might as well walk together," she said in a pleasant voice.

"Well . . ." Lucy began. If there was one thing she *didn't* want to do, it was to walk home with the woman who was going to take Clipper away. And besides, if she walked with Miss Sullivan, it would look as though she really were teacher's pet.

Lucy thought fast. "I'm not going home right now, Miss Sullivan," she said. "I promised to meet Sarah at the drugstore for a soda."

It was a lie. Lucy knew that Sarah had hurried home to help her parents in the store. She would be working there for the rest of the afternoon.

"Oh, well, I understand," Miss Sullivan said, nodding. "We can walk together another time." She turned and headed down the road toward Lucy's house.

"Now what do I do?" Lucy muttered as she stood alone outside the schoolhouse, clutching her books and her lunch pail. "I can't go home yet because *she'll* be there. But I have to go somewhere."

She thought for a moment. Then she decided she would go to the drugstore after all. "By the time I finish my soda and get back home, Miss Sullivan will probably be gone," she told herself as she walked into town. "How long can a driving lesson take, anyway?"

When Lucy got to the drugstore, she ordered a chocolate-and-vanilla soda with whipped cream and a cherry from Mr. Bean, the druggist. She sat at a little glass-topped table by the window and waited for him to bring it over to her.

When the soda arrived, Lucy sipped it slowly. The soda tasted so creamy and delicious that Lucy began to feel more cheerful. Maybe Mr. Turner is right, she thought. Anything can happen in two weeks. Maybe Papa will hate driving the car and decide to sell it back to Miss Sullivan.

Lucy finally finished her soda. She stood up, dug into her pocket, and pulled out a nickel. She took the empty glass over to the counter and handed it to Mr. Bean, along with the nickel. "Thank you, Mr. Bean," she said. "That was delicious!"

She picked up her books and lunch pail and stepped out the door. She had just started up the street when she heard a car horn go "ah-ooga" behind her. She turned and saw her father and Miss Sullivan driving down the street toward her. Lucy's father was at the wheel. As they passed Lucy, they grinned at her and waved.

Lucy's face fell. She had to admit that her father looked as if he was having a very good time driving the new car. Clipper was as good as gone.

Lucy Takes a Ride

On Friday morning at breakfast, Lucy's father said, "Miss Sullivan and I want to take you for a ride in the car today, Lucy. You haven't been out with us yet, and I feel bad that you're missing all the fun."

Lucy nearly choked on her piece of cornbread. Every day that week, she had made sure she was the first person out the door as soon as Miss Sullivan dismissed the school. She would hurry home and go straight up to her room or to the paddock to visit Clipper. So far, she had been able to avoid seeing Miss Sullivan at the house.

Lucy took a drink of milk to wash down the piece of cornbread. Then she said, "I'd, um, like to go with you, Papa, but I was planning to ride Clipper after school. He really needs the exercise."

Grandma Gordon gave Lucy a sharp look that make her feel uncomfortable. Lucy know that her grandmother had seen her riding Clipper the day before. But Grandma Gordon didn't say anything.

"Well, then, we'll come by after my lesson and pick you up," Lucy's father said with a smile. "You should be finished with your ride by then."

If only I can think of a way to make my ride last until dinnertime, Lucy thought. But how?

She came up with a plan as she was walking to school. She would ride out to Cherokee Lake. The lake was ten miles away, but it was a straight and easy ride all the way down the main road. By the time she reached the lake and returned home, it would be too late to go driving with her father and Miss Sullivan.

When Lucy got home after school, she headed for the paddock. As usual, Clipper came over to welcome her.

"Are you ready for a nice long ride, Clip?" she asked him, as she stepped through the gate. She took hold of his halter and led him out of the paddock to the barn.

There, Clipper stood quietly and patiently while she saddled and bridled him. Next, she placed a little stepstool next to him. She climbed up onto the stepstool, put her hands on the pommel, and put her foot in the stirrup. Then she swung herself into the saddle.

"Right, Clip, here we go!" Lucy said. She reached over and patted his neck. Then she lightly touched his sides with her legs.

Lucy walked Clipper up the path to the road and turned him in the direction of Cherokee Lake. As she did, she caught a glimpse of Miss Sullivan walking toward the Gordons' house from the opposite direction.

Lucy urged Clipper into a running walk and then settled herself comfortably in the saddle to enjoy the smooth and easy glide of his pace. No one had taught Clipper this special, fast-moving gait. He had been born knowing how to do it.

Lucy let him run for a while before she urged him into his special canter. The Walker's canter was a high, bounding gait, as smooth as his running walk, but faster. It made Lucy feel as if she were riding in a rocking chair instead of on a horse.

They were about five miles from the lake when Lucy suddenly spotted a group of men and wagons blocking the road ahead. As she slowed Clipper down and rode closer, she could see men hauling logs down

a mountain road into the wagons. Lucy recognized
Marcus Sloan as the man supervising the log haulers.
He saw her riding toward them and walked over to
her. He was a short, muscular man with a deeply
tanned face and the same curly, reddish-gold hair as
his daughter Emily.

"I hope you weren't thinking of going any farther,"
he said, as Lucy brought Clipper to a stop. "My men
will be hauling these logs for another hour at least."
He gave Clipper a pat, adding, "I heard that your father
bought a car and wants to get rid of Clipper. I'd be
interested in buying him. I could use another cart
horse, and Clipper would be perfect."

That Emily Sloan, Lucy thought furiously. What a
blabbermouth. And she didn't even get her facts
straight!

"I'm sorry, Mr. Sloan," she said coldly. "But Clipper
is already spoken for." Without another word, she
turned Clipper around.

"Well, if your father changes his mind, tell him to
phone me up," she heard Mr. Sloan call out as she
started back up the road.

Lucy shuddered at the thought of Clipper working
as a cart horse, hauling a wagon full of logs. For the
first time she was almost thankful that Clipper was
going to someone like Miss Sullivan. "But I still don't

want you to go away at all," she whispered to Clipper.

When she reached her house, she saw the car parked out in front. But there was no sign of her father or Miss Sullivan.

"Maybe Papa's lesson is over, and he and Miss Sullivan decided not to go for a ride with me," Lucy said hopefully to herself. "So it's safe to come home."

Just as she was turning Clipper onto the path, she saw Miss Sullivan come out of the house, followed by Lucy's father and Grandma Gordon. All of them were laughing.

"Now, Maggie," Lucy's father was saying. "You can't make me believe that you've never tasted fresh buttermilk before!"

"But it's true, Phillip," Miss Sullivan insisted. "I'm a city slicker, remember?"

"Well, if you thought buttermilk tasted good, wait until you try Mother's buttermilk biscuits at the church social tomorrow night," Dr. Gordon said.

"I'll look forward to that," Maggie replied. She took Grandma Gordon's hand. "Mrs. Gordon, thank you so much for preparing such a delicious snack," she said warmly. "But you really shouldn't have gone to all that trouble."

"Nonsense, Maggie," Grandma Gordon said in a gruff voice, but with a pleased expression on her face.

"The apple pie was just sitting there, waiting to be eaten."

"And the buttermilk was just waiting for Maggie's first taste of it," Lucy's father said. He and Miss Sullivan smiled at each other and then burst out laughing again.

I think I'm going to be sick, Lucy thought. Why are Papa and Miss Sullivan acting so foolish? And when did they start calling each other by their first names?

Just then, the three adults spied Lucy sitting there on Clipper, watching them.

"Perfect timing," Lucy's father said with a grin. "Now we can go for our car ride."

"But Papa, what about Clipper?" Lucy asked. "He has to be brushed and watered."

"I'll do that," Grandma Gordon offered. She stepped up to Clipper and held out her hand for the reins. After a moment's hesitation, Lucy slid down off Clipper's back. Then she handed the reins to her grandmother.

"Right," Lucy's father said. "Let's go!"

He walked over to the car and pulled open the door. "After you, my dear," he said to Lucy.

Lucy stepped into the front seat of the car. But before she could sit down, her father said, "I think you'd better sit in the back, Lucy. I need Maggie up front to make sure I'm driving the car correctly."

Lucy squeezed through the narrow space and sat down on the hard leather seat. Her father got into the driver's seat and pressed a lever to the left of the wheel. "I'm moving the spark lever up and down," he reported to Miss Sullivan, who got out and stood in front of the car. "Now I'm going to open up the throttle."

He glanced over his shoulder at Lucy. "This is how you start up a Model T," he said to her.

"But nothing is happening," Lucy said.

"It will," Lucy's father told her. He pressed a lever to the right of the wheel. At the same time, Miss Sullivan turned a big crank attached to the front of the car. All of a sudden, the engine jumped to life, and the car began to chug and shake.

"We're off!" Lucy's father said. The car jerked

forward a few times, then stopped. "That darn clutch,"
he muttered.

In the back seat, Lucy folded her arms across her
chest and waited for her father and Miss Sullivan to
start up the car again. This isn't very much fun, she
thought. We're not going anywhere!

Miss Sullivan and Lucy's father started up the car
once more. This time, Dr. Gordon managed to control
the clutch and keep the car moving at a steady pace.
"It really is easy, once you get the hang of the clutch,"
he said to Miss Sullivan as they drove toward Main
Street. He pulled the throttle out a little more, and the
car picked up speed. "Now we're really cooking. We're
going thirty-five miles an hour!"

Just then, Lucy spotted a horse-drawn wagon
pulling out of a side road into the middle of Main
Street several yards ahead of them. There was a coop
of chickens in the back of the wagon. The car sped
closer to the wagon, but Lucy's father didn't slow
down. Instead, he reached out the window and
squeezed the horn several times. Lucy covered her
ears at the loud sound.

The driver of the wagon turned his head, and his
eyes opened wide at the sight of the Model T barreling
toward him. He quickly steered his horse out of the
way, and Lucy's father zipped past him, still honking

the horn. As they went by the wagon, Lucy glanced at the chickens. They were screeching, flapping their wings, and fluttering around the coop. A couple of chicken feathers landed in Lucy's lap.

Dr. Gordon pulled back on the throttle and stepped on the brake to slow the car down. But he forgot to press down on the clutch at the same time. The car slowed down, but then it came to a dead stop next to the sidewalk.

Several boys who were playing with marbles on the sidewalk nudged one another and pointed to the car. One of the boys cupped his hands to his mouth and called out, "Get a horse!"

Lucy definitely agreed with him.

"I'm sorry, Maggie," Lucy's father said apologetically. "I should have been paying more attention to the brake and the clutch."

"That's all right, Phillip," Maggie told him gently. "It takes time to learn how to drive a car." Patiently, she began to explain what he had done wrong and how he could correct it. Lucy's father listened to her carefully.

Lucy sat silently in the back seat as her father and Miss Sullivan talked quietly together. Dr. Gordon had put his right arm around the back of Miss Sullivan's seat. Lucy felt left out and forgotten.

Papa only cares about Miss Sullivan, she thought bitterly. I might as well not even be here. I wish I'd never agreed to take a ride in this dumb car!

CHAPTER SIX

Lucy's Great Idea

After what seemed like forever to Lucy, her father and Miss Sullivan finished their conversation. Dr. Gordon turned around and smiled at Lucy. "Well, my dear, are you enjoying your first ride in the car? Wasn't I right when I said that you would love the car once you rode in it?"

Lucy knew that he would be disappointed if she told him how she really felt, so she just nodded and said in a quiet voice, "It's fine, Papa."

"Oh, Phillip, I just remembered something," Miss Sullivan said suddenly. "Your mother asked us to pick up some cinnamon at Wilkes's store."

"I'll go," Lucy offered eagerly. She couldn't wait to

get out of the car and into the warm, friendly store with Sarah and her parents. Lucy's father handed her a quarter. She stood up and waited as he worked the door handle.

"It seems to be stuck," he said, jiggling the handle. "Just a minute now. There! I've got it!" He pushed open the door. Then he sat back in his seat.

"Papa," Lucy said. "I can't get out of the car until you move the seat."

"Oh," Dr. Gordon said, sitting up quickly. "That's right." He eased himself out of the car and reached down. This time he was able to find the correct lever.

Lucy wriggled her way between the seats and began to step down out of the car. But the step was high, and she had forgotten how far it was to the ground. She lost her balance and had to grab onto the door handle to keep from falling. She looked up at her father. He was busy talking to Miss Sullivan and hadn't seen her almost fall.

Sighing, Lucy turned, hurried down the sidewalk to Wilkes's store, and ran up the front steps. When she entered the store, she saw Sarah's mother standing behind the counter, chatting with Dr. Adam Grant, the town vet. Lucy liked Dr. Grant very much. He was a handsome, friendly man with black hair and blue eyes. He was known in Pine Bluff as an excellent doctor who loved animals and was very gentle with them.

Both Mrs. Wilkes and Dr. Grant smiled at Lucy.

"How's that beautiful Walker of yours?" Dr. Grant asked. "Did he catch that cough that's been going around?"

Lucy shook her head. "Clipper's just fine, Dr. Grant," she replied.

"Sarah's upstairs doing her homework, honey," Mrs. Wilkes told her. The Wilkes family lived in an apartment above their store. "But I'm sure she'd be happy to take a break and visit with you for a little while."

"I'll see Sarah tomorrow night at the church social," Lucy said. "I just came in to buy some cinnamon for Grandma. Papa and Miss Sullivan are outside waiting in the car."

Just then, Mr. Wilkes poked his head out of the entrance to the storeroom. "I'll have your order ready in about twenty minutes, Dr. Grant," he said. "Will that be all right?" He smiled at Lucy and waved.

"That will be fine, John," Dr. Grant told him. Mr. Wilkes nodded and disappeared into the storeroom. Dr. Grant chuckled. "I always seem to run out of everything at the same time."

"Oh, you bachelors are all alike," Mrs. Wilkes said teasingly. "You really ought to find a nice young woman and get married. A wife would help you keep track of what's in your pantry." She opened a canister on the shelf behind her and began to scoop some cinnamon into a little paper bag. "Will four ounces be enough, Lucy? I know your grandma likes to use a lot of cinnamon in her recipes."

Lucy didn't answer at once. An idea had just come to her. Dr. Grant wasn't married, and neither was Miss Sullivan. What if she could somehow introduce them to each other? Maybe they would fall in love. Then Miss Sullivan would leave her father alone. But how could she arrange for the two of them to meet?

"Lucy?" she heard Mrs. Wilkes say. She blinked and turned to Sarah's mother. "Four ounces?" Mrs. Wilkes repeated.

Lucy nodded. "Oh, yes, Mrs. Wilkes, that will be fine."

"Are you going to the social, Dr. Grant?" Mrs. Wilkes asked as she weighed the bag of cinnamon.

"I certainly am," Dr. Grant said, smiling. "I wouldn't miss it for the world. The only thing that would keep me away is if one of my patients needs me. That's what happened before the last social."

The social! Lucy thought excitedly. That would be the perfect place to get them together. "Our new teacher, Miss Sullivan, is going to the social, too," she

said. "Have you met her yet, Mrs. Wilkes? She's very pretty and nice."

"I've met and talked to Miss Sullivan several times," Mrs. Wilkes said. "She often comes into the store. I like her very much, and so do the children at school, I hear."

"Maggie Sullivan is the nicest and loveliest woman I know," Dr. Grant said warmly. "And one of the smartest, too. I'm very much looking forward to seeing her at the social."

"Here you are, Lucy," Mrs. Wilkes said, handing her the small bag of cinnamon. Lucy put the quarter on the counter, took the bag, and waited while Sarah's mother rang up the sale and gave her fifteen cents change.

"Thank you, Mrs. Wilkes," Lucy said, pocketing the change. She was about to leave the store when she remembered her manners. She turned and added politely, "It was nice seeing you again, Dr. Grant."

"Same here, Lucy," Dr. Grant said with a grin. "And I hope you'll dance a dance with me at the social."

"I sure will," Lucy said, smiling shyly.

Her smile widened as she left the store and skipped down the steps to the sidewalk. From the way Dr. Grant had talked about Miss Sullivan, Lucy was positive that he liked her very much. It should be as easy as pie to get them together at the social, she thought. Now if I could only find a way to make Miss Sullivan give up Clipper.

The trip home in the car was a little smoother than the trip into town. Lucy's father only stalled out once, next to the schoolhouse. Lucy knew Miss Sullivan rented the little schoolteacher's house in back of the school.

After Miss Sullivan helped start up the car again, she said, "I'm sure you can make it home without any more trouble, Phillip. Why don't I just get out here? That will save you the bother of walking me home. It's nearly six o'clock, and I'm sure Mrs. Gordon is expecting you and Lucy home for supper."

"Why don't you have supper with us, Maggie?" Lucy's father suggested. "I know Mother and Lucy will be tickled pink. Right, Lucy?"

The last thing Lucy wanted was for Miss Sullivan to come over for supper. But she kept her thoughts to herself. Out loud she said in a polite tone, "Yes, we would like it very much if you came over, Miss Sullivan." Maybe she won't come, Lucy thought hopefully. Maybe she'll say she's too busy.

"Well, I do have spelling tests to correct," Miss Sullivan said. "But I guess they can wait."

"Good!" Lucy's father said with a grin, as he

adjusted the throttle. "And I promise not to stall the car again on the way home."

After they had reached the house and gotten out of the car, Dr. Gordon took Miss Sullivan's arm and escorted her into the house. Lucy headed down the path to the paddock to take Clipper back to the barn.

The sun was setting, and there was a rosy glow over the meadow. Clipper stood out like a black velvet shadow against the fading light. Lucy watched him for a moment, her heart filled with love and pride. Then she stepped into the paddock, tiptoed up to him, and stroked him gently.

"Are you ready for some supper, boy?" she said softly. She took hold of his halter and led him to the barn.

While Clipper was eating his pail of oats, bran, and apples, Lucy spread a soft, deep bed of clean straw in his stall. Next, she filled a pail of water from the trough and brought it into the barn. When he was finished eating, she slipped off his halter.

She had just given him a hug and a kiss, when she heard Grandma Gordon call out her name. With a sigh, she left the barn and slowly walked toward the house. This was one meal she was not looking forward to.

Lucy washed her hands at the kitchen sink and

stepped into the dining room. Everyone was already seated at the table. Lucy saw that Miss Sullivan had been placed next to Grandma Gordon.

"Now that Lucy's here, you may carve the ham, Phillip," Grandma Gordon said. Then she looked at her granddaughter, her eyes twinkling. "Well, Lucy, how do you think I did with Clipper? Did he look all right to you? Lucy doesn't trust anyone to look after Clipper except herself," she added to Miss Sullivan. "Even though I was taking care of horses long before she was born."

"He looks beautiful, Grandma," Lucy said sincerely. "You did a wonderful job. Thank you."

"Speaking of Clipper," Lucy's father said as he handed a plate of ham to his mother, who passed it along to Miss Sullivan. "According to our agreement, you're planning to take ownership of him and the buggy a week from Saturday. That's right, isn't it?"

Lucy's stomach turned over. Oh, no, she thought miserably. Please don't talk about taking Clipper away. Anything but that.

"Yes," Miss Sullivan said, nodding. "But I have to admit that I've been so busy with the school, I haven't had time to think about Clipper and the buggy. And there's something else I ought to confess, too." She paused for a moment. Then she said with an apologetic laugh, "The fact is, I really don't know much about horses, coming from the city and all. I need to find someone to teach me how to ride, drive, and care for Clipper. I don't know how long it will take to learn those things, but I feel I should do it before Clipper comes to live with me."

Lucy couldn't believe what her father said next.

"Why, that's no problem, Maggie," he said with a smile. "Lucy knows everything about riding, driving, and caring for Clipper. She'll be happy to give you lessons. Won't you, my dear?"

CHAPTER
SEVEN

High Hopes

The rest of the meal seemed to Lucy to go by in a blur. She barely touched her food. But neither her father nor her grandmother said anything about it. They were too busy laughing and chatting with Miss Sullivan.

"Lucy, why don't you take Maggie out to the barn so that she and Clipper can get acquainted," Lucy's father said after they had finished dessert. "I'll help your grandmother clear the table."

Without a word, Lucy got up from the table and led Miss Sullivan through the kitchen to the back door. They stepped outside and walked down to the barn together in silence. Lucy knew that it was rude of her not to try to make conversation with a guest, but she didn't care.

After they stepped into the barn, it was Miss Sullivan who spoke first. "Oh, I recognize him now," she said as they stopped in front of Clipper's stall. "He was the horse that ran away after my car backfired at the parade." She looked at Clipper, frowned, and shook her head. "I don't know, Lucy," she said in a doubtful tone. "A horse that gets spooked that easily might be high-strung and hard to handle."

It was clear to Lucy that Miss Sullivan didn't know anything about horses, especially Tennessee Walking Horses. An idea suddenly flashed into her head. What if I can make Miss Sullivan believe that Clipper is the wrong horse for her? Then maybe she won't want him after all.

"I know what you mean," Lucy said, stepping into Clipper's stall. Clipper immediately nickered softly, turned, and began to gently nuzzle Lucy's hand. Out of habit, Lucy began to stroke his muzzle. She had to admit that he wasn't acting very high-strung. But somehow she had to convince Miss Sullivan that he usually was.

"He's acting gentle now," she told Miss Sullivan. "But you never know when he'll act up. Just the other day, when I was trying to hitch him up to the buggy, he wouldn't let me near him. He shies away from other horses on the road, too. And sometimes he kicks when you try to lead him out of his stall." She looked at Clipper, who blinked lazily at her. "Yes, he certainly can be skittish," Lucy added, trying to make her voice sound as if she was exasperated with him.

Miss Sullivan stood there silently for a moment, watching Clipper and biting her lip. Then she looked at a little gold watch pinned to her blouse.

"It's time for me to go home," she said. "Thank you for being so honest with me about Clipper, Lucy. Perhaps I should think about whether or not he's the right horse for me."

"Oh, yes," Lucy said seriously. "I would think about it very carefully, if I were you."

Miss Sullivan smiled at Lucy and gave her arm a friendly squeeze. "I'll see you at the social tomorrow night, dear." Then she turned and walked out of the barn.

Lucy felt a little uncomfortable as she watched Miss Sullivan go. Never had she told so many lies. She leaned her head against Clipper's soft neck and whispered. "But I had to do it, Clip. It might be the only way to keep her from taking you away from me."

The next morning brought a nice surprise for Lucy. As she was sitting at the table eating her scrambled eggs, her father said, "I need to visit some of my patients at their homes today. Would you like to go with me, Lucy?"

"Oh yes, Papa," Lucy said, her eyes shining. "I'd love to go!" She felt very happy. It had been a while since the two of them had spent any time alone together.

Then she remembered something, and her face fell. "Are we driving in the car, Papa?" she asked.

"No," her father said with a laugh. "I don't feel quite ready yet to drive the car by myself. Almost, but not quite. We'll take Clipper and the buggy. I've already hitched him up, and your grandmother has packed a picnic lunch. Then, after my rounds, we'll drive over to Bean's Drugstore and have a soda, just like we always do."

Lucy grinned with delight. "That will be wonderful, Papa!"

After breakfast, the two of them headed out to the buggy. Lucy was carrying the picnic basket, and Dr. Gordon was carrying his black medical bag. Lucy's father carefully placed the basket and bag on the back seat of the buggy, unhooked the reins, and stepped into the driver's side. Lucy climbed into the buggy and settled herself cozily in the seat next to him.

"Who are we visiting first?" she asked, as her

father guided Clipper onto the road.

"Charlie Turner," her father replied. "He broke his arm a few days ago while mending the roof of Billy Deakins's barn. He lost his footing and fell off the roof. Luckily, he landed in a hay wagon. I saw him at the hospital, but I want to make sure his arm is knitting properly."

He turned Clipper onto a winding mountain road. There were ruts in the dirt road that had been made by the steady traffic of logging wagons and deepened by rainstorms. But Clipper didn't seem to mind the ruts. He moved up the road with his usual gliding walk.

Lucy breathed in the cool, fresh mountain air and looked contentedly at the sun-dappled leaves of the elms and maples they passed. Up here, the trees were beginning to flame into color, and their red, orange, and yellow leaves stood out against the dark green of the pines. Lucy felt as though she were a million miles away from Model-T cars and Miss Maggie Sullivan.

Soon Lucy could see a little log cabin up ahead. Charlie Turner was sitting on the porch steps smoking a pipe. As they drove closer, Lucy saw that Mr. Turner's left arm was in a sling. Andy Jackson sat next to him. As soon as the dog saw Clipper coming toward the cabin, he padded down the steps and trotted over to greet him.

Dr. Gordon brought Clipper to a stop in front of the cabin, and he and Lucy stepped out of the buggy. Lucy reached down to give Andy Jackson a pat on the head. The big yellow dog wagged his tail and pushed his nose into her hand. Then he went over to Clipper and lay down beside him. Lucy walked over to Mr. Turner.

"I see that you and Clipper decided to visit me and Andy Jackson for a change," Mr. Turner said with a smile. "How are things going?"

Lucy smiled back at him. "I'm keeping my hopes up, like you said," Lucy told him.

"Good girl," Mr. Turner said with a nod.

Lucy's father came over and placed his bag on one of the steps. Then he sat down next to Mr. Turner. "How's the arm, Charlie?" he asked. "Been giving you a lot of pain?"

Lucy sat on the bottom step and leaned against the railing. She folded her arms around her knees and watched as her father began to examine Mr. Turner's arm. She noticed how gentle he was, and how patiently and carefully he listened to Mr. Turner's answers to his questions.

"It's healing nicely, Charlie," Dr. Gordon said when he had finished his examination. "But you'll need to

keep the sling on for at least another week. Then I'll
look at it again. Meanwhile, I wouldn't do any heavy
work, if I were you."

"I guess that doesn't include dancing," Mr. Turner
said, his eyes twinkling. "I'm intending to claim your
ma for at least five dances tonight at the social."

"I'll tell her that," Lucy's father said with a laugh.
"She's looking forward to dancing with you, too."

Lucy and her father waved good-bye to Mr. Turner
and got back into the buggy. Lucy's father steered
Clipper back down the road. When they reached the
main road again, they took a turn up another
mountain road to visit Dr. Gordon's next patient.

After they had visited two more patients, Lucy's
father stopped Clipper in a grassy mountain meadow
beside a stream. He unhitched the Walker and led him
down to the stream for a drink. Then he tied Clipper
to a picket line and let him graze while he and Lucy
sat in the buggy and ate their lunch.

"Who's your next patient, Papa?" Lucy asked, as
she munched on a ham sandwich.

"Mrs. Preston," her father replied. "She's my last
patient today. She and her husband live in a cabin not
too far from here."

"I remember them," Lucy said. "Mr. Preston is a
farmer. I went with you to visit him a few times after

he broke his leg. I signed his cast."

"That's right," Lucy's father said. "Mrs. Preston is pregnant, and her baby is due any day now. She's a little nervous because it's her first baby."

When they had finished their lunch, Lucy's father hitched up Clipper again, and they drove to the Prestons' farm. Lucy saw Mr. Preston standing in front of the house, twisting a big straw hat in his hands.

"I'm so glad you're here, Doctor," he said anxiously. "Martha's real worried and upset. She's imagining all sorts of terrible things about having the baby."

Lucy's father put his arm around Mr. Preston's shoulders. "You need to calm down, too, Tom," he said quietly. "Having a baby is a natural, normal part of life. I can understand why Martha feels scared, but she's a healthy young woman, and nothing should go wrong. Can you help me try to convince her of that?"

Mr. Preston gulped and nodded. Then he and Lucy's father went into the house together. At the door, Dr. Gordon turned to look at Lucy. He didn't have to say anything. Lucy understood exactly what his look meant. She nodded and said, "I'll stay outside with Clipper this time, Papa." She knew that her father needed to talk to Mr. and Mrs. Preston alone.

Lucy sat in the buggy and waited. Soon she began

to feel drowsy, so she lay down on the seat. A moment later, she was fast asleep.

She woke up just as her father was coming back to the buggy. Lucy sat up and rubbed her eyes. "Is everything all right?" she asked with a yawn.

"I think so," her father said, stepping into the buggy. "I gave Mrs. Preston some exercises to do that will relax her. The calmer she is, the easier her baby's delivery will be." He looked at his watch. "I didn't think I'd have to spend so much time here. I'm afraid we won't be able to stop for our soda after all, Lucy. I have to get back home. Maggie is expecting me for my driving lesson."

Lucy looked down at her lap with a sulky expression. It had been a perfect day, and now Miss Sullivan had ruined it. Once again, she hoped she would be able to get Dr. Grant together with Miss Sullivan at the social so that she could get that woman out of her life for good!

At the Church Social

Lucy sat on a bale of hay in the big barn used by the church for its social. She had been at the party for an hour, and there was still no sign of Dr. Adam Grant.

"Maybe one of his patients got sick after all," Lucy murmured with a sigh. "It would be terrible if he didn't show up."

"What would be terrible?" Sarah asked. She was sitting next to Lucy, swinging her legs in time to the fiddle music.

Lucy leaned over and whispered her plan about Miss Sullivan and Dr. Grant into Sarah's ear. Then she drew back and said anxiously, "You won't tell any of the other girls, will you, Sarah? They would tease me to death if they knew."

"I'm not a tattletale," Sarah insisted indignantly. "Besides, we're best friends, aren't we? Best friends always stick together."

"Right," Lucy said with a grin. She looked around the room again. On one side was a huge table crowded with good things to eat and drink. Opposite the table on the other side of the room was a platform. On the platform stood four musicians. Two of them were playing fiddles. One was plucking at a bass fiddle, and the fourth was playing an accordion. In the middle of the room, couples were lined up opposite each other, dancing and clapping to the strains of a Virginia reel. Lucy saw her father and Miss Sullivan dancing together.

"How are you going to get Dr. Grant and Miss Sullivan together?" she heard Sarah ask.

Lucy had thought about that during the buggy ride to the social. "I've got it all worked out," she told Sarah. "When Dr. Grant asks me to dance, I'll say I promised that dance to Papa. Then I'll tell him that Miss Sullivan needs a partner. I'm sure he'll dance with her."

As soon as the reel ended, Charlie Turner hopped up onto the platform and held up his hand to quiet the crowd. "If you folks have any notion of resting after that reel, you can forget about it," he called out. "You came here to dance, and dance you shall. Ladies and gentlemen, take your partners for the square dance!"

"Come on, Lucy," Sarah said eagerly. "Let's be partners." She grabbed Lucy's hand and pulled her into the middle of the floor. Soon they were joined by Mr. and Mrs. Wilkes. As the four of them formed a square, Lucy glanced over and saw her father and Miss Sullivan standing by the food table. He was handing Miss Sullivan a plate of food.

Just then, the fiddlers started to play, and Mr. Turner began to call out the dance. "Bow to your partner, swing and sway. Promenade left and shout 'Hooray'!"

Lucy tried to keep her mind on Mr. Turner's calls during the dance, but she kept looking toward the barn door to see if Dr. Grant had arrived yet.

She saw him come in while she and Sarah were doing a do-si-do. She stopped short, and Sarah bumped into her. "Lucy," Sarah hissed. "What are you doing?"

"He's here," Lucy whispered. She watched as Dr. Grant stepped over to Mr. Bean and began to chat with him. She knew she couldn't put her plan into action until the square dance was over, so she turned back to Sarah and her parents and listened more carefully to the calls.

When the dance had ended, Lucy saw Dr. Grant head across the room to where her father and Miss Sullivan were standing. She followed him over. When he reached Miss Sullivan, he grinned and said, "Hello, Maggie."

Miss Sullivan turned, and her eyes lit up with pleasure. "Adam!" she exclaimed. "It's wonderful to see you!"

Then, to Lucy's amazement, Dr. Grant put his arms around Miss Sullivan and gave her a big hug and a kiss. Lucy looked at her father. He was smiling at Dr. Grant and Miss Sullivan. The three of them began to talk and laugh together. Lucy was completely baffled. She couldn't understand why Dr. Grant and Miss Sullivan were acting like such good friends, and why her father didn't seem to mind.

Just then, the band swung into a waltz. Dr. Grant spotted Lucy and stepped over to her, smiling.

"Would you like to dance?" Dr. Grant asked her. "Or would you rather sit this one out with a glass of punch?"

"I'd like some punch, please," Lucy said. Together they walked over to the table.

"You know, I'm really glad Maggie took my advice

and decided to accept the teaching position in Pine Bluff," Dr. Grant said, as he ladled punch into a small glass and handed the glass to Lucy.

"But I don't understand," Lucy said in a confused tone. "Did you know Miss Sullivan before she moved here?"

"We grew up together in Richmond," Dr. Grant told her. "Maggie is my cousin." He turned and watched Miss Sullivan and Lucy's father dancing together. "I must say that she looks much happier now than she did in Richmond. Especially now that she's found a nice beau like your father."

No wonder they acted so friendly with each other, Lucy thought. They're related! She looked down at her punch glass in glum silence. She felt terrible that her plan hadn't worked.

The dance ended, and the band immediately began to play another waltz. Lucy recognized it as the one her father always danced with her.

"Excuse me, Dr. Grant, but I have to find my father now," she said. "We always dance this waltz together."

She put down her punch glass and made her way through the crowd to her father. But when she reached him, she saw that he was dancing with Miss Sullivan again. With a sigh of disappointment, she turned and headed back to the bale of hay to sit with Sarah. Then she saw that Sarah was dancing, too. Her partner was the mayor's twelve-year-old son, Bert. Dr. Grant was leading Mrs. Bean onto the floor. Even Grandma Gordon was dancing, with Charlie Turner.

Suddenly Lucy couldn't stand to be in the room a moment longer. She turned and ran out of the barn to the tree under which Clipper was standing. Andy Jackson was curled up on the ground next to him.

Lucy put her arms around Clipper's neck and buried her face in his mane. She felt sadder and lonelier than she ever had before. "All I have is you, Clipper," she whispered. "And I won't have you much longer."

Just then she heard someone softly call out her name. She raised her head and saw Miss Sullivan coming toward her.

"I saw you leave," Miss Sullivan said. "I know how hard it can be when everyone else is having a good time, and you're not."

Lucy didn't know what to say, so she just nodded.

Miss Sullivan sat down on the bench by the tree and folded her hands in her lap. She looked down at her hands for a moment. Then she looked up at Lucy. "You know, we're going to be studying family trees soon," she said. "Can you tell me something about your mother?"

"There really isn't much to tell," Lucy said, surprised at Miss Sullivan's question. "Her name was Victoria, and she died when I was three years old. I have a picture of her in a locket. Papa and Grandma Gordon say I look like her, but you can't tell from the picture in the locket." She paused for a minute. Then she said, "I remember one time, when I was sick, she held me in her arms and sang to me. It was a lullaby, I think. I remember that after she sang it to me, I started to feel much better."

"You must miss her very much," Miss Sullivan said gently.

Lucy nodded. Then she asked, "Where are your folks, Miss Sullivan?"

"Both my parents died when I was a baby," Miss Sullivan told her. "Until I was ten, I was brought up in an orphanage."

"That's so sad," Lucy said. She felt very sorry for Miss Sullivan, and deep down she knew that she didn't hate her anymore.

"Yes, it's sad," Miss Sullivan agreed. Then she smiled. "But the year I turned ten, I was adopted by wonderful people, a United States senator and his wife. Their love and support have meant a great deal to me. I'm happy now, Lucy. Really."

She stood up and stepped over to where Lucy was standing. She reached out and timidly touched Clipper's muzzle. "It's hard to believe that such a gentle-looking horse could be so moody," she said.

Lucy knew she couldn't lie to Miss Sullivan any longer. She took a deep breath and said, "Clipper isn't high-strung at all, Miss Sullivan. He just got scared at the parade because your car backfired. Any horse would have behaved like that. I made up all those stories about his acting skittish, too." Her eyes filled with tears. "It's going to be so hard to lose Clipper," she said, her voice trembling. "I love him so much. I lied to you because I just didn't want you to take him away. Can you understand that?"

"Oh, Lucy, dear," Miss Sullivan said softly. "I am so sorry. I had no idea how you felt about Clipper. Of course I understand. If it had been me, I would have acted the same way."

Just then, Lucy's father came up to them. "What are you two doing out here?" he asked. "I've been looking all over for you, Lucy. The last dance is starting in a minute, and I was hoping you'd dance it with me. It's a waltz."

"I'd love to, Papa," Lucy said. Miss Sullivan took out her handkerchief and gently wiped the tears from

Lucy's cheeks. Lucy smiled at her, and Miss Sullivan smiled back.

"Let's go, Papa," Lucy said. Her father put his arm around her, and together they walked back into the barn to dance the last dance.

After the social had ended, the Gordons and Miss Sullivan piled into the buggy for the drive home.

"Well, did everyone have a good time?" Lucy's father asked, as he steered Clipper in the direction of the schoolhouse.

"Yes, if you call dancing four waltzes, two polkas, and one reel with Charlie Turner fun," Grandma Gordon said as she reached down to rub her tired legs. "I don't know where that man gets his energy!"

Dr. Gordon laughed. Then he said, "You know, Maggie, I think I've got the hang of the car, and I can drive it by myself now. Instead of coming over to give me a driving lesson on Monday after school, why don't you and Lucy begin your lessons on Clipper?"

He pulled into the schoolhouse drive and stopped the buggy in front of Miss Sullivan's house.

Lucy noticed that Miss Sullivan hadn't said a word since they had left the social. She wondered why Miss Sullivan was so quiet.

"Monday will be fine," Miss Sullivan said, speaking for the first time. As she got out of the buggy, she added, "Thank you for a lovely time." With that, she turned and walked toward the house.

Lucy felt tears welling up in her eyes again. If Miss Sullivan had agreed to come over on Monday for lessons on Clipper, it could only mean one thing. She was going to take Clipper away after all.

The Storm

66T oday's the big day," Lucy's father told Lucy and Grandma Gordon at breakfast on Monday morning.

"The big day for what, may I ask?' Grandma Gordon said, as she handed her son a plate of pancakes.

"It's the day I make my rounds for the first time by car instead of by buggy," Dr. Gordon said enthusiastically. "I'll be able to visit more patients in one morning than I could before in a whole day!"

"But, Papa, it was so much fun on Saturday, when you and I drove in the buggy together to visit your patients—wasn't it?" Lucy asked.

"Yes, it was," her father agreed, smiling at her. He looked thoughtfully at her for a moment, and then he asked, "Do you remember the first time you ever came with me on my rounds?"

"I remember," Lucy said, nodding. "I was five years old, and it was wintertime."

"It was the coldest winter in twenty-five years, the paper said," her father went on. "Your grandmother didn't think you should go with me because it was so cold."

"With good reason," Grandma Gordon added in her crisp voice. "The child came home with a nasty cold. But, as usual, you were as stubborn as a mule and insisted that she go."

"I took a wrong turn, and we found ourselves at the edge of a pond that was frozen over," Lucy's father continued.

"I remember!" Lucy exclaimed. "You wanted Clipper to drive us across the pond, but he balked and wouldn't do it."

"That's right," her father said. "I even tried leading him across the pond on foot, but he wouldn't budge. I was mad as thunder at that horse, until I found out later that the ice on the pond was too thin. We would have fallen right through it."

"And Clipper somehow knew that," Lucy finished.

"Clipper is smart, Papa. That's one of the reasons I love him so much." She looked at him and said in a pleading tone, "Please don't give Clipper away to Miss Sullivan, Papa."

Her father sighed deeply. "Lucy," he said quietly. "You think I don't understand how you feel about Clipper, but I do. But a bargain is a bargain. I simply cannot go back on my word."

Disappointed, Lucy got up from the table. She would never be able to convince her father to let Clipper stay with her. Six days from today, Clipper would be gone forever.

"It looks as though there's going to be a storm," Grandma Gordon said, as Lucy was leaving the room. "I think you'd better wear your oilskin slicker and your rainhat."

"All right, Grandma," Lucy said obediently. She went to the hall, pulled her slicker and hat out of the closet, and put them on. Then she picked up her books and lunch pail and left the house.

It wasn't raining yet, but as Lucy walked toward the schoolhouse, she noticed thick black clouds scudding across the sky. As she walked, the sky grew darker and darker. By the time she caught up with Sarah, Faith, Carrie, and Emily outside the schoolhouse, a cold wind had begun to blow.

All four girls were wearing slickers and hats like Lucy's. Emily was carrying a big umbrella, too. She pointed her umbrella at a group of boys who were tossing a ball around to one another.

"Just look at those boys," she said scornfully. "Why would anyone want to run around chasing a ball in this weather?"

"Well, at least they're keeping warm," Faith said with a shiver. "Let's not wait for the bell. Let's go inside now."

They all trooped into the schoolhouse. In the back of the room, Miss Sullivan was lighting a fire in the big coal stove. A number of students were already seated at their desks.

"I hope this stove will warm things up," Miss Sullivan said, as she straightened up and clapped the coal dust from her hands. "Why don't you girls take your seats, and I'll ring the bell."

Lucy and her friends got out of their slickers and hung them on the hooks next to the door. The bell began to ring, and a few moments later, the boys stepped inside, one by one.

When everyone was seated and quiet, Miss Sullivan gave out assignments to each class. Lucy noticed that all the children in the first class were absent, and so were many from the second class.

Their folks probably kept them home because of the weather, she thought.

As the morning wore on, Lucy wished that she had stayed home, too. The wind was blowing hard, and every so often, the schoolhouse would shudder and creak. Lucy fidgeted in her seat. She tried to concentrate on the grammar lesson Miss Sullivan had assigned to her class, but the noise of the wind seemed to drown out her thoughts.

Lucy was worried about Clipper, too. She had turned him out into the paddock before breakfast. Would Grandma Gordon remember to take him back in the barn if there was a bad storm?

By noon, the wind was howling fiercely, and it had begun to rain. The coal stove couldn't keep the schoolroom warm, and everyone was shivering.

At noon Miss Sullivan closed the grammar book and announced, "Before this storm gets any worse, I think we should all go home."

In the dim light of the room, Lucy and her schoolmates picked up their books and retrieved their lunch pails. They put on their slickers and went out the door. Lucy quickly said good-bye to Sarah and then started up the road. It was slow going. She was walking against the wind, and the rain was pouring down. Lucy was glad her grandmother had made her wear her slicker and hat. But by the time she was halfway home, her thin leather boots were soaked through. The gusty wind blew the rain into her face, and once or twice she was almost knocked off her feet. Several times she had to stop to catch her breath.

Finally, she saw the house up ahead. The car was parked in front. Her father had come home from his rounds. Lucy decided that he was probably sitting in the warm dining room having lunch.

There was nothing Lucy wanted more than to dash into the safe, warm house. But first she had to make sure that Clipper was all right. She hurried down the path to the paddock. She breathed a sigh of relief when she saw that he wasn't out there in the wind and the rain. She knew that Grandma Gordon or her father must have taken him to the barn, but she wanted to see for herself.

Using all her strength against the wind, she pulled open the barn door. She stepped inside and saw Clipper in his stall. He was calmly drinking from a pail of water.

"Clipper," Lucy called out softly. The Walker raised his head and whinnied a welcome. Lucy put her books and lunch pail down on the floor and went over to him. She gave him a hug and said, "This storm isn't bothering you one bit, is it, Clip?" Clipper nodded his head up and down. "I'm glad you agree with me," Lucy said with a laugh. She patted his neck, then turned and left the barn.

As soon as Lucy walked into the house, she ran upstairs to her room and changed her shoes. Then she went back downstairs into the dining room. Her father and grandmother were sitting at the dining-room table eating lunch.

"I suppose Maggie decided to close school because of the storm," Lucy's father said when he saw his daughter come into the room. "That was a smart idea."

Lucy sat down at the table and opened her lunch pail. Grandma Gordon had just poured her a glass of milk when the telephone in the hall began to ring.

Lucy's father wiped his mouth with his napkin, stood up, and left the room to answer it.

"Dr. Gordon here," Lucy heard him say into the phone. "Hello? . . . Hello? . . . Speak up, please, I can't hear you. What's that? . . . I understand. I'm on my way. Don't worry."

A few minutes later, he returned wearing his slicker. "That was Tom Preston," he told Lucy and Grandma Gordon. "Heaven knows how he managed to get to a phone. He's sure that Mrs. Preston has started her labor. I'll be back soon as I can."

"Oh, Phillip, must you go in this weather?" Grandma Gordon asked anxiously. Lucy was thinking the same thing.

Lucy's father laughed. "I have to go, Mother. I'm a doctor, remember? Besides," he added, "I'll be driving the car. There's nothing to worry about." With that, he turned and left the room.

Lucy finished her lunch and helped Grandma Gordon clear the table and wash up the dishes. Then she settled herself in the big chair by the fireplace and began to read her new book, *Anne of Green Gables.* She glanced out of the window and saw that the wind had died down, and the rain had stopped. The sky looked brighter, too. The storm had ended.

Now Papa will have an easier time getting to Mr. and Mrs. Preston's house, she thought with relief. She went back to reading her book. The next time she looked up, she glanced at the clock on the mantelpiece. An hour had gone by since her father had left.

Lucy was about to return to her story, when something caught her eye. There, in the far corner of the room, was her father's black medical bag. He must have forgotten it in his hurry to get to the Prestons. Her father would need his bag, of that Lucy was sure. She thought for a minute. Then she put down her book and went into the kitchen. Grandma Gordon was standing over the table mixing the batter for a cake.

"Papa forgot his bag," Lucy said.

"That man would forget his head," Grandma Gordon said. "I hope he can manage without it."

"What if he can't? I'm going to take Clipper and bring it to him," Lucy said.

"It's too dangerous, Lucy," Grandma Gordon protested. "With all this rain, there may be mud slides."

Lucy smiled. "Don't worry, Grandma, I'll be perfectly safe. I'll be riding Clipper, remember?"

She hurried out the kitchen door before Grandma Gordon had the chance to say another word.

Clipper to the Rescue

Ten minutes later, Lucy was riding Clipper at a running walk down the road. The road was full of puddles, but Clipper didn't seem to mind. He glided through them, kicking up very little water.

Soon they reached the mountain road Lucy and her father had taken on Saturday. Lucy turned Clipper onto the muddy road and slowed him to a walk. Together they followed the winding road past dripping trees heavy with rain. Clipper picked his way through the mud with ease.

At the top of the hill, the road branched off in different directions. Lucy stopped Clipper for a moment and looked at the roads in confusion. "One of them goes to the meadow where Papa and I had our lunch," she said with a frown. "And beyond the meadow is the road that leads to the Prestons' farm. But which of these roads do I take?"

Just then, to Lucy's amazement, Clipper began to move forward, toward the road at the right. Lucy didn't try to stop him. After all, maybe he did know the way.

Clipper had followed the road for about half a mile when Lucy suddenly spotted her father's car. It was sitting in the middle of the road. As she and Clipper came closer, she could see that the car was stuck in the mud. Lucy passed the car and looked inside. Her father wasn't there.

"He must have gone ahead on foot to the Prestons," Lucy told herself.

She and Clipper continued up the road. Just as they rounded a bend in the road, Lucy saw her father sloshing through the mud.

"That dang car," Lucy heard him mutter. "It wasn't supposed to get stuck like that!"

"Papa," Lucy called out. "I've brought your bag!" She waved it above her head. Dr. Gordon turned, and a look of relief came over his face.

"Am I glad to see you!" he exclaimed as Lucy rode up to him. "Hurry! There's no time to lose!"

Lucy slid down off Clipper while he swung into

the saddle. Then she handed the medical bag to him and stuck her foot in the stirrup. She held onto her father's belt and pulled herself up behind him. As soon as she was in the saddle, she clasped her arms around her father's waist to steady herself.

"Ready?" Dr. Gordon asked.

"Yes, Papa," Lucy replied. She felt Clipper move forward.

When they rode into the meadow, Lucy's father told her, "Hold tight, Lucy. I'm going to take him across the meadow at a canter."

Lucy tightened her grip around her father's waist as he urged the Walker into a canter. But even though Clipper was moving fast, and Lucy was perched on the back of the saddle, she wasn't jarred a bit.

At the edge of the meadow, Dr. Gordon slowed Clipper down and turned him onto the road where the Prestons lived. They arrived at the house a few minutes later.

Tom Preston came running over to them as they were dismounting. "I think the baby's coming, Dr. Gordon," he said excitedly.

"All right, Tom," Lucy's father said calmly, as he tied Clipper to the porch railing. "Why don't you heat up some water for us. Lucy and I will take care of things with Martha."

Together, he and Lucy went into the house. When they stepped into the bedroom, they saw Martha Preston lying in the bed. Dr. Gordon walked over to her and took her hand.

"Now, Martha," he said gently. "I'm here to help you deliver your beautiful new baby."

The young woman smiled weakly.

At that moment, Tom Preston came into the room. "The water's ready, Dr. Gordon," he said. "It's in a basin in the kitchen."

"Good," Lucy's father said with a nod. "Lucy, why don't you go in the other room and keep Tom company."

Lucy sat on a straight-backed chair and tried to make polite conversation with Tom Preston, but she could tell he wasn't really listening. Every few minutes, he'd jump from his seat and pace up and down the floor of the small cabin, his face strained with worry. Lucy was watching him pace the room for what seemed like the thousandth time, when she heard a high-pitched wail coming from behind the closed door. Tom Preston gave a sigh of relief and sank into the nearest chair just as the door opened.

Lucy looked over and saw her father holding a newborn baby, swaddled tightly in a towel. Dr. Gordon placed the small bundle in Tom Preston's hands. "Well,

Tom," he said. "You and Martha have a beautiful baby daughter. And if she's as sweet and spunky as my Lucy, you'll be happy parents indeed!"

Lucy blushed with pleasure at her father's compliment.

Tom Preston nodded. "I don't know how to thank you, Dr. Gordon," he said sincerely. "You were wonderful. You too, Lucy."

"I think it's Clipper we should be thanking," Lucy said. "After all, he got us here!"

After Lucy's father had given Tom Preston some instructions on how to care for his wife, he and Lucy left the house. They mounted Clipper and started down the road again. As they passed the car, Lucy asked, "Are you going to try to pull it out of the mud, Papa?"

"Not now," her father replied. "The car can wait. I want to get you and Clipper home."

They rode on in silence for a while. When they reached the barn, Lucy's father said thoughtfully, "Clipper has done a fine day's work. And I learned an important lesson. I realize that a horse can be just as important as a car. Especially when the horse is Clipper." He looked at Lucy and shook his head. "I'd keep both Clipper and the car if I could," he said with a sigh. "But I don't see how I can go back on my word to Maggie. It wouldn't be fair."

Just then, Miss Sullivan stepped into the barn. "I thought I'd find you two here," she said with a smile.

"I suppose you've come for your riding lesson on Clipper," Dr. Gordon said to Maggie.

"Well, yes," Miss Sullivan said softly. "But there's another reason, too." She turned to Lucy. "I would like to learn how to ride and drive Clipper. But I know now that I can't take him away from you."

Lucy gazed at Miss Sullivan, her eyes shining with joy. "Do you really mean that?" she asked.

"Of course I do," Miss Sullivan assured her. "I plan to buy another horse soon, and when I do, I want to learn everything I need to know about horses. Will you teach me, Lucy?"

"Oh, yes," Lucy said with a grin. "I'll be happy to teach you."

Lucy's father shook his head. "I can't let you do this, Maggie," he said. "We made a bargain. By rights, Clipper belongs to you."

"Clipper will never be mine," Miss Sullivan said gently. "He's Lucy's horse. And your horse, too. He always has been, and he always will be."

She put her hand on his arm, and her eyes twinkled at him merrily. "Phillip Gordon, I can be as stubborn as you can. My mind is made up. You can't change it. Besides," she added with a smile, "I already have my eye on a horse for sale. I discovered yesterday that Mrs. Atkins, the mayor's wife, wants to sell Misty. And she's asking a very reasonable price."

Lucy's father stood there silently, biting his lip. "All right," he said suddenly. "I'll agree to keep Clipper if you'll let me buy Misty for you."

"Agreed," Miss Sullivan said, holding out her hand. She and Lucy's father grinned at each other as they shook hands.

"Oh, thank you, Papa," Lucy said joyfully. "Thank you, Miss Sullivan. This is the best day of my life!"

"It's a pretty special day," her father agreed. "I learned that there's room in the world for new inventions and for old ways, too."

"And I found out that there's room for new friends, like Maggie," Lucy said, smiling shyly as she used Miss Sullivan's first name.

Suddenly, she heard Clipper nicker and felt him nudge her shoulder. "I guess Clipper's feeling a little left out," she said in an understanding tone. She turned and gave him a hug. "Old friends are wonderful, too, Clipper," she whispered to him. "Especially friends like you."

Then she looked at Maggie Sullivan, smiled, and said, "Are you ready for your first lesson?"

FACTS
ABOUT THE BREED

You probably know a lot about Tennessee Walking Horses from reading this book. Here are some more interesting facts about this uniquely gaited American breed.

∩ Tennessee Walking Horses generally stand between 15 and 17 hands. Instead of using feet and inches, all horses are measured in hands. A hand is equal to four inches.

∩ Tennessee Walking Horses are usually black or chestnut, although any solid color is acceptable. They often have prominent white markings.

∩ Tennessee Walking Horses have very thick manes and tails. Both the mane and the tail are left long and flowing.

∩ The breed has a short back, strong limbs, and powerful hind quarters.

∩ Tennessee Walking Horses were developed in the state of Tennessee in the mid-19th century. The breed's foundation sires, or fathers, were the stallion Black Allen, whose father was a Standardbred and whose mother was a Morgan, and his son, Roan Allen. Thoroughbred, Narragansett Pacer, and Saddlebred blood also contributed to this smooth-walking breed.

∩ In the early days of the breed, the horses were known variously as Southern Plantation Walking Horses, Tennessee Pacers, Walkers, and Nature's Rocking Horses. They were also called Turn-Rows because they could turn between the rows of small growing crops without damaging the plants.

Ω Although the Tennessee Walking Horse Breeder's Association wasn't established until 1935, the Tennessee Walker really gained the spotlight in 1932. That year, the Tennessee Valley Authority, which brought electricity to much of rural Tennessee, lighted night horse shows that focused on Tennessee's unique breed.

Ω The Tennessee Walking Horse Breeder's Association of America was founded in Lewisberg, Tennessee, in the spring of 1935. Since that time, approximately 300,000 Tennessee Walking Horses have been registered with the association. Now called the Tennessee Walking Horse Breeders' and Exhibitors' Association, the headquarters for the breed is still located in Lewisberg.

Ω The Tennessee Walking Horse's most outstanding feature is the running walk. It is said that riding a Walker at the running walk is like gliding on a magic carpet. Like the regular, flat-footed walk, the running walk is a four-beat gait. When moving in a running walk, the horse moves one foot while keeping the other three feet on the ground.

∩ While executing a running walk, the Tennessee Walking Horse tucks its hind quarters under. The hind foot glides as much as 18 inches beyond the point where the front foot left the ground. This placement of the hind hooves is called the *overstride*. The overstride is what makes the running walk so smooth.

∩ The overstride also makes the running walk a fast gait. A Tennessee Walking Horse can travel at a running walk as fast as 15 miles per hour, although the usual speed is between 6 and 9 miles per hour. The horse can keep moving at this comfortable pace for hours.

∩ The horse is so relaxed while doing the running walk that its head nods, its ears flop, and its teeth click like castanets!

∩ The running walk is not the Tennessee Walking Horse's only special gait. The canter is also renowned for its smoothness and is said to feel just like a rocking chair.

∩ The Tennessee Walking Horse is known as a "bounce free" horse. This has made the breed an excellent and comfortable pleasure horse. In addition, the horse is known for its sweet temperament. The Tennessee Walking Horse is so calm that hunters can shoot at birds while mounted.

∩ Today the Tennessee Walking Horse is used primarily as a show or pleasure horse under either English or Western tack. The horse will also work in harness, pulling carriages. In addition, this breed has been known to compete in both jumping classes and barrel races.

♪ Because of their calm temperament and ease of handling, Tennessee Walking Horses are used in mounted police units in cities. They also work as mounts for forest rangers in state and national parks.